# Charles Perrault
# Best Known Fairy Stories

# Retold by Lornie Leete-Hodge

Illustrated by Ronald Embleton

**DEAN**

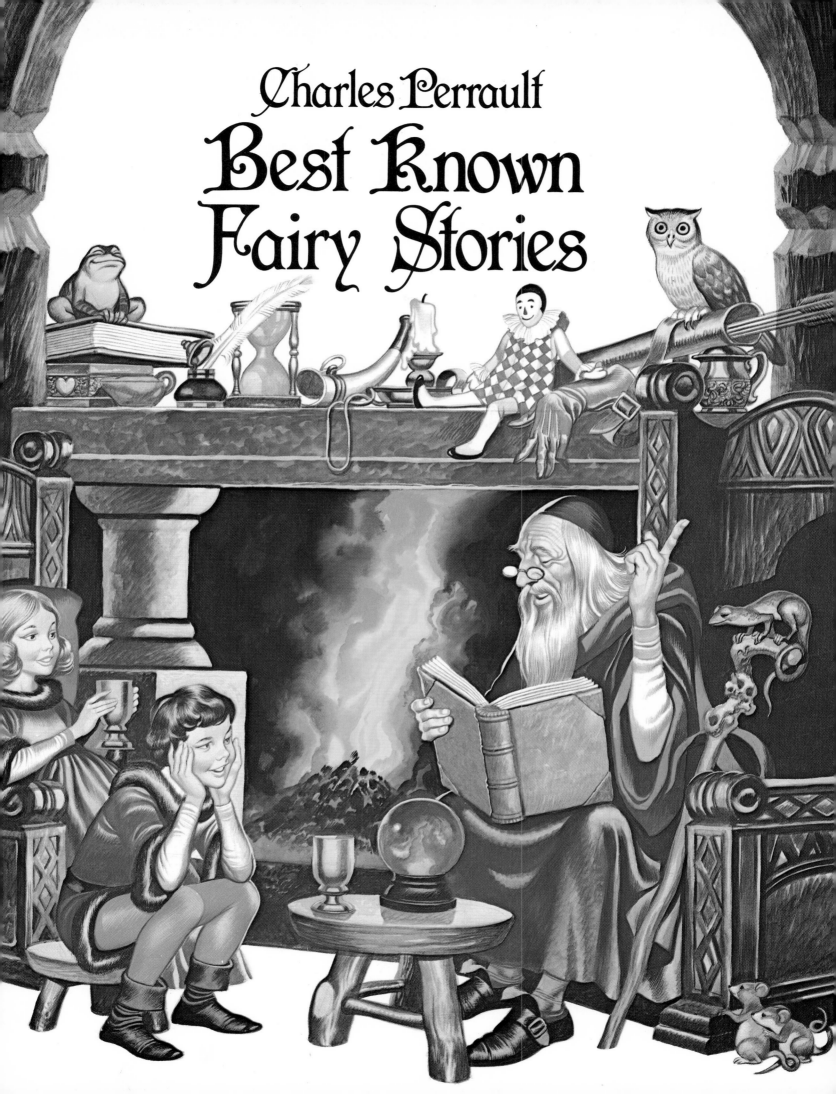

# Charles Perrault
# Best Known Fairy Stories

Originally published in England by Dean & Sons, Ltd.
Published in United States and simultaneously in Canada by Joshua Morris, Inc.
431 Post Road East
Westport, CT 06880
Copyright © The Hamlyn Publishing Group, Ltd. 1983
All Rights Reserved

ISBN 0-887-05057-3

Made and printed in Great Britain by
Purnell and Sons (Book Production) Ltd.,
Member of the BPCC Group, Paulton, Bristol

# Contents

# Puss in Boots

Long, long ago, there lived a poor old miller. All he had in the world were three sons, a donkey and a cat. And of course his mill. When he died, he left the mill to the eldest son. He left the donkey to his second son. And his youngest son, Tom, received the ginger cat. Poor Tom was very sad. He looked at the cat and, after scratching his head, said, "Well, I'd best make a pie of you and sell the skin!"

The cat looked at him. Then, to his great surprise the cat spoke.

"Don't do that, Master," he said. "Just give me what I ask, and I will soon make your fortune. You will have riches far greater than your brothers. Just bear with me."

"Oh well, I've nothing to lose," said Tom. "If it doesn't work, I can still eat you and sell the fur. What do you want?"

"First of all, I'd like a pair of high boots—red leather I think would be best, or do you think blue with my red fur?"

"Boots? If you want boots, Puss, I think they'd better be blue as your fur is red. Anything else?" And he bowed low, mocking the cat.

"I'd like a fine hat with a sweeping feather, and a small sack. Nothing too large, as I have to carry it."

Tom looked at the cat who was very serious. "Oh well, I'll spend my last pennies on you," said Tom. "Then it's up to you."

So he asked the shoemaker to make a fine pair of blue soft leather boots for Puss. Then he bought him a large hat with a curly feather. Puss put them on, and preened and primped in front of the pond where he could see himself in the water. "Don't forget the sack," he called stretching in the sun. He loved his boots. They were just right.

"Here you are, one sack!" said Tom throwing it down. "Now what?"

"Wait and see. Leave it to me," said Puss.

He set off across the fields in his fine new boots and feather hat. Everyone now called him Puss in Boots and he felt very proud. But he was a clever cat, and knew just how to help his master. He put some lettuce and bran in the sack, then hid out of sight. Very soon two silly rabbits found the food, and Puss jumped out and snared them in no time.

Tossing his catch over his shoulder, Puss set off for the King's palace. He knocked on the door and asked to see the King at once. The King was surprised that a cat wanted to see him and told his guards to let him in. Puss bowed low.

"Your Majesty!" he said, sweeping off his hat with a flourish. "Your Majesty, I bring you a gift from my master, the Marquis of Carabas!" And he gave the King the fine, succulent rabbits he had caught. The King was delighted. There was nothing he liked better than rabbit pie.

Puss went home, well pleased. His plan to give Tom a new name had worked well.

Every day for a week, Puss took a present to the King. One day it would be a choice salmon or trout (poached from the King's own river!), another day, a plump partridge or a hare, and so on. The King, who loved his food, was very grateful. Puss told the King that his master, the Marquis of Carabas, had sent the presents.

While at Court, Puss listened to all the talk and gossip. He quickly learned that the King had a beautiful daughter. He heard they were going for a drive next day by the river, and scampered home across the fields to make his plans.

"Master, Master," he called, "come and listen to my plans for tomorrow. You must go and bathe in the river at noon. Do exactly as I tell you, and our fortunes will be made."

So, next day, exactly at noon, Tom went swimming in the river. He heard carriage wheels rumbling along the road, the jingle of harness and the scrunchy breath of the horses. "Stay there," Puss hissed at him

and ran along the road to meet the coach. "Help! Help!" he cried, waving his hat, "oh please help me. My master, the Marquis of Carabas is drowning!"

The King ordered the coach to stop, and his footmen helped Tom from the water. "Someone has stolen his clothes!" shouted Puss, so the King told the men to bring a suit from the Palace for the Marquis. In fact, crafty Puss had hidden Tom's clothes under a stone. If his plans failed, he would go back for them later.

When the Princess saw the handsome Tom, dressed in fine clothes, she fell in love with him, and begged the King to let him ride in the coach. So Tom climbed in and held hands with the Princess and looked at her and he stopped wondering what would happen next.

Puss ran on ahead. In a field, he saw some reapers hard at work and called out to them.

"The King is coming this way! When he asks you who owns these fields, tell him they belong to the Marquis of Carabas. If you don't you'll be thrown into prison."

So the reapers promised and went on with their work. Soon the King and his daughter, with Tom beside them, came along the road. Leaning out of the window, the King called out, "Who owns these fine fields?"

9

"The Marquis of Carabas," replied the reapers, bowing low.

On ahead, a few miles, Puss saw some men making a hayrick. "The King is coming," he called, "and when he asks you whose rick it is, tell him it belongs to the Marquis of Carabas. If you don't, you'll be thrown into prison!"

So, when the King saw the fine, high rick, he stopped the coach and asked the men whose it was, and was told it belonged to the Marquis of Carabas. Now the King was greatly impressed, for this young man must be very wealthy to own all this land and fine hayricks, and have so many workers on his estates.

Meanwhile, Puss had reached a fine castle high on a hill. A fierce ogre lived there, and everyone was frightened of him. In fact, he was the real owner of all the lands Puss had claimed for the Marquis of Carabas. Puss rang the doorbell, tugging at the great chain and hearing its echo throughout the castle. "Let me in," he told the servant, "I must see your master at once."

"What is it, what do you want?" the ogre asked crossly. He hated everyone and did not want to see anyone at all.

"The King is coming, he wants to meet you," said Puss. "He wants to meet the largest landowner in the kingdom."

The ogre was flattered when he heard this news. "Tell me more," he said, inviting Puss to sit down.

"I've heard so much about you," said Puss, "but, seeing you, I am sure it is all lies."

"Lies! Lies! What do they say about me?" thundered the ogre, towering above Puss.

Secretly, Puss was a tiny bit scared, the ogre was so big and ugly!

"Oh, just lies," he said, "lies about you!"

"Tell me what they say," bawled the ogre, "how dare they tell lies about me. Tell me, and I will cut their tongues out!"

"They say," said Puss, leaning forward and whispering, just a little, "they do say you can turn yourself into a lion! But I don't believe a word of it." And he tilted back in his chair.

"You don't believe it!" screamed the ogre, "watch this!" In a trice, he had turned himself into a fierce lion and stood roaring and menacing on the floor beside Puss.

Puss made himself sit still. After all, a lion is only a big cat, he told himself, and he twirled his hat defiantly.

"Oh, very good," he said, "so you *can* turn yourself into a lion. They weren't telling lies after all. Except, maybe, oh well, they must have

been when they said you could do other things."

"*Other* things!" the ogre nearly exploded. "What do they say?"

"Just that you can turn yourself into small animals as well," said Puss, "but I don't believe it. How can such a big, fierce lion turn into a tiny thing, such as a mouse, for instance?" And he waited, anxiously.

The ogre gave a low growl.

"What did I tell you?" said Puss. "It's impossible."

"Nothing, but nothing, is impossible for me," roared the lion. "Watch!" And before Puss could move, the great roaring lion turned into a tiny mouse at his feet. Wasting no time, Puss pounced on the mouse and ate him up in one gulp! That was close! Dusting his whiskers, for he was a polite cat, he ran out into the courtyard to await the King's arrival.

"Welcome to the castle of the Marquis of Carabas," he said, bowing low and sweeping off his fine hat. "Welcome to the castle!"

The King and Princess were delighted to see the Marquis lived in such a fine castle. Tom was pleased as well!

"Will Your Royal Highnesses honour our humble castle by joining us for supper?" Puss asked. "Nothing special, just a little meal." And he showed the way to the dining hall. A great feast had been prepared for the ogre, and Puss knew it would not disappoint the King and Princess.

"This is magnificent," said the King, looking round him at the fine old castle, its walls lined with shields and battle axes, the trophies won by the ogre.

Feeling content with his magnificent feast, and knowing his daughter had eyes for none but Tom, the King asked Tom if he would like to marry the Princess. Tom could not believe his ears, but he accepted at once, for he loved her.

Soon the old castle rang with the celebrations for the wedding and Puss made all the arrangements. Tom and his Princess lived happily ever after, but Tom never told his wife the secret of the Marquis of Carabas. As for Puss, he lived in luxury and never caught another mouse. The taste of that ogre had put him off mice for ever!

13

# Sleeping Beauty

**O**nce, long years ago, there lived a King and Queen who were sad because they had no children. Then at last their prayers were answered and the Queen had a daughter. Everyone in the whole kingdom rejoiced, the bells pealed, and there was dancing in the streets.

The King ordered that a huge Christening feast be prepared. He invited the kings and queens from other lands, the nobles and ladies of his own kingdom, and, as the very special and honoured guests, the six fairies who lived in his kingdom and watched over it. They would be the child's godmothers, and he hoped they would bestow gifts on her.

The great banqueting hall was prepared. All the finest silver and gold were laid on snowy-white tablecloths, and garlands of flowers hung from the rafters. Never had the hall looked so beautiful. The centre table was golden, and, for the special guests, each fairy had been given a specially-made golden casket with her own spoon, fork and knife, all in gold and set with diamonds, rubies and emeralds. No one had ever seen such fine presents before, but this was a very special day.

The musicians played and everyone was sitting down to the feast when the door opened, and a very old, very gnarled and bent fairy came into the room, leaning on a stick. She was dressed in black from head to foot and was very angry.

"Where is my invitation?" she screamed, pointing her stick at the King who rose to his feet in horror.

"You did not invite me," she said slowly and loudly. "Why?"

"But, we, that is, we . . ." the King stammered and sat down, feeling very afraid.

The truth was, no one had seen the fairy for so long, for she lived hidden away in her cave, that everyone thought she was dead. They had forgotten all about her.

"Quick, set a place for the fairy," ordered the King, but of course there was no room at the centre table. There was no golden casket, no golden spoon or knife and fork set with jewels for her. The old fairy glowered. She had been slighted, and she muttered threats between her teeth as she picked at the feast. Everyone was unhappy. Somehow, her coming had cast a blight over the festivities. One of the young fairies, who sat near, tried to offer the old fairy her golden casket, but she pushed it aside and mumbled into her soup. After the feast was over, the young fairy thinking the old one might give the baby an unlucky gift hid behind some curtains to watch what happened. That way she could be the last to present a gift and might be able to mend any evil the old fairy might do.

The great moment had arrived. One by one, the fairies came up to the magnificent cot on which the tiny princess lay asleep and offered their gifts.

"May she be the most beautiful princess in the world!" said the first and touched her with her magic wand.

"May she have the nature of an angel," said the second, stooping to touch her.

"May she have grace," said the third, giving a gentle touch with her wand.

"May she have feet that dance to perfection," said the fourth skipping forward to touch the Princess with her wand.

"May she sing like a nightingale," crooned the fifth fairy touching her with her wand.

Then, the old, wicked fairy hobbled up to the cot, and looked down at the Princess, still asleep. She was shaking with rage. Leaning heavily on her stick, she pointed a bony hand towards the cot, her wand held in a claw-like grasp.

"One day, one day, little Princess, you will pierce your hand with a spindle and die!"

And she touched the sleeping child with her wand and gave a fierce, gloating cackle. Then she drew her black cloak tightly around her and stumped off, muttering to herself.

A gasp of horror ran through the room. What a terrible gift for the baby! Everyone held their breath.

Then the youngest fairy stepped out from her hiding place behind the curtains.

"Take heart," she said, smiling at the weeping King and Queen, "the Princess will not die. It is true that I have no power to break the evil fairy's spell, and your daughter will prick herself with a spindle when she is fifteen. But, instead of dying, she will only fall into a deep sleep that will last for a hundred years. When that time has passed, a king's son will come and wake her."

And she bent down and touched the sleeping child with her wand to seal her promise.

Anxiously the King and Queen ordered that every spindle in the country must be destroyed. Somehow, the terrible fate of the Princess must be averted. On pain of death, the King forbade anyone to use a spinning wheel or keep a spindle in their house. So all spinning ceased and the looms were silent.

The years passed happily and the wicked fairy's decree was forgotten. The other fairies' promises came true and the Princess grew up into a lovely girl who could sing and dance beautifully and everyone loved her. One day, when the Princess was fifteen, she and her parents were visiting one of their castles in the country. She was happy and running about, exploring the castle. She had never seen one as old as this, and wanted to see every little room and corner.

"Oh what is this?" she cried when she saw a tiny, twisting stairway, and she ran up to a small garret at the top of a tower. She stopped outside a door. From within, she could hear a strange whirring sound. She had never heard it before. She pushed open the door and there sat an old woman bent over a spindle, spinning a few threads. She had not heard the King's orders forbidding the use of spinning wheels, and sat all day long spinning.

"Oh, what are you doing?" asked the Princess, staring at her.

"Just spinning," said the old woman. She did not know the Princess.

"What is that?" asked the Princess, "No one has told me of spinning! May I try it?" And she moved towards the old woman.

The old woman turned. "It's very easy," she said, handing the Princess the spindle. No sooner had she picked it up, than she pricked her hand and fell into a deep swoon! The wicked fairy's wish had come true.

The old woman was very alarmed. She cried out for help and tried

to lift the Princess and wake her. The King and Queen, hearing the noise, came running. They knew it was too late. The servants threw perfumed water on the sleeping Princess and shook her but she slept on and on. It was all to no avail.

Sadly, the King and Queen ordered that the Princess be carried on a litter and they returned to their home. The King asked that the Princess be laid in her bedchamber on a bed embroidered with gold and silver and she looked beautiful as she lay asleep. Her lips were still red and her cheeks pink.

"She must sleep until the spell breaks," said the King and wept. The good fairy who had saved her life by changing the evil fairy's wish that the Princess should die, was away when the spell came true. A little dwarf, wearing seven league boots, ran to tell her, and she flew at once to the castle riding high above the clouds. "It is all right," she said, trying to comfort the weeping King and Queen. Then she thought how lonely the Princess would feel when she woke up after a hundred years and found she was alone. She picked up her magic wand.

Gently, and swiftly she touched everyone in the castle. First the King and Queen, all the ladies and gentlemen of the Court, the officers, the soldiers, the servants, the maids, the pages, the pastrycooks, no one was forgotten. Outside she touched the great horses that pulled the carriages, the gentle ponies, the cows, the sheep, the pigs, the watchdogs and the cats. Last of all, she touched the dancing butterflies. Everyone was soon asleep, even Barney, the Princess' little dog, who had climbed up on to her bed to be with his mistress.

There was a great, great silence. Everyone fell asleep at once and there was no sound at all, anywhere. Time stood still. Within a few minutes, an enchanted forest grew up, thick and brambly all round the castle hiding it from view. No one would see the castle and find out its secrets, not for a hundred years.

So the years passed. Then at last, the time came. One day, a

handsome Prince and his friends were riding near the castle. They had had fine sport with their hunting and wanted to find somewhere to stay for the night. The Prince looked all around and could just see some towers peeping out above a great wood.

"What is that place?" he asked. No one knew.

"It's an ogre's palace," said one of his friends, "he steals children. Let's keep away."

Then, a bent old peasant came along. "Young master," he said, bowing low, "more than fifty years ago, I heard my father tell the story that there was a beautiful princess in that old Castle. She must sleep for a hundred years until some prince woke her up. Some spell or other. That's all I know." And he shook his head.

"No harm in looking!" said the Prince. What excitement! There might be a beautiful Princess behind all the bramble in that castle.

"Don't be too disappointed," laughed his friends. They did not believe one word of the story.

"I'll see if I can get through," said the Prince picking up his sword and hacking his way through the brambles. It was hard work until he cleared the outer ones, then the others fell away as if by magic. Before he knew it, he was inside the great courtyard. Here, the Prince was filled with a strange foreboding. Everywhere was silent. Nothing moved. There was not a sound in all the world. There were men, women and animals, all lying down, all asleep. Gingerly, he crept forward, sword in hand. This was odd indeed. Even the cups they held were filled with wine, fresh and sparkling and not a drop had spilled.

Plucking up his courage, the Prince went on, pushing open the great

door which creaked on its hinges. Here, more people lay sleeping.
Every room was the same. Bravely, the Prince shook a pageboy, trying
to wake him, but the boy never stirred. In the kitchens, the cooks sat
with ladles in their hands, some with a half-plucked chicken on their
laps, the feathers never stirring, not even when he blew at them.

Up and up the long staircase the Prince climbed. He opened first
one door, then another, until at last he came to a beautiful room with a
red curtain pulled half across. In a bed embroidered with silver and
gold lay the most beautiful girl he had ever seen. At the foot of the bed,
a small dog lay sleeping.

The Prince put out his hand and touched her face, but she did not
move.

"Wake up!" he said, shaking her. But she went on sleeping.

The Prince was speechless. How could he wake this lovely Princess? The old man's words were true, but what use to him? He bent down and kissed this beautiful girl. It seemed she must sleep for ever, and he had best be on his way.

As his lips touched hers, the spell broke and the Princess' eyes fluttered and she stirred. Soon, she was wide awake and sat up. That was the signal for everyone in the Castle to wake up, and the air was filled with the bustling sounds of people working and singing. The little dog began to bark at the stranger.

"Shush, Barney," laughed the Princess, "don't make such a noise!"

Then she laughed. Fancy telling him to be quiet when he had not barked for a hundred years!

The King and Queen came hurrying into the room and kissed the Princess. They thanked the handsome Prince for rescuing them from the wicked fairy's spell. As for the Prince, he was very happy, for soon, he decided, he would marry the most beautiful Princess in all the world!

# The Fairy

**O**nce upon a time a widow lived with her two daughters. The elder was proud and bad tempered, just like her mother. But the younger girl was kind and good, and one of the prettiest girls in the whole land.

Life was hard for the younger daughter. Her mother did not care for her. She made her do all the housework, while the elder girl sat and sulked all day.

One morning, the mother spoke to her younger daughter. "Go and fetch the water from the well," she said, "and look sharp about it!"

This meant a long walk of about a mile. The well was near the edge of the woods and the road to it was hard and dusty. "Hurry along now and don't dawdle," her mother scolded as the young girl set out.

"Of course, Mother," she promised smiling, "I will be as quick as I can."

The girl set out carrying the wooden bucket and singing as she walked. She nodded to the flowers that grew at the wayside, and spared a word for the rabbits and birds in the hedgerows. On reaching the well, she lowered the bucket and was just pulling it up, winding with the long handle, when an old woman limped up to her.

"Can you spare a drop of water for an old woman who is hot and tired?" she asked, settling herself down stiffly.

"Gladly, there's plenty here," said the girl. "Sit there, and I will bring you some in a moment."

To make sure the old woman had the freshest, coolest water, she plunged the bucket down again, deep into the bottom of the water, even though it meant a long haul to get it up again. The bucket was filled with the coolest, freshest water when it came to the top. The girl steadied the bucket and lifted it very carefully. She did not want to lose a drop. She took a small jug from the side of the bucket, filled it, and walked over to the old woman.

"Here you are, this will refresh you," she said. "And if you want any more, tell me, and I will draw up some more for you."

"Thank you, my child," said the old woman when she had had enough, and handed back the jug.

"Are you sure you have had all you want? It's no trouble to draw up some more," said the girl smiling.

"You are a kind girl," said the old woman, "to help someone like me. I will give you a gift. Every time you speak, flowers and jewels will fall from your lips."

"Oh, there's no need for any thanks," laughed the girl, "you are welcome to a drink at any time. Good day to you. Take care."

She waved goodbye to the old woman and set off along the hot and dusty road with her heavy bucket. As she walked, the bucket grew heavier and she changed it from one hand to the other. She smiled to herself. What an idea! Fancy jewels and flowers falling from her lips, all for a drink of water!

"And where have you been?" shouted her mother as she came to the cottage. "Loafing and wasting time I'll be bound, and here I am waiting for the water! I told you not to dawdle. You just never listen. Well, give it here girl, I haven't all day." And she shook her head at the girl.

"I'm sorry, Mother. There was this strange old woman at the well. I gave her a drink of water."

"You've no time to go giving drinks of water to beggars," her mother was saying when she stopped, her hand to her mouth in amazement. For, as her daughter spoke, diamonds and flowers fell from her lips. Her mother and sister picked them up. What was this? They couldn't be real! But they were. The flowers were sweet-smelling and the diamonds winked in the sunlight. They had never seen anything like it!

"Tell me again," said her mother, "who did you meet at the well?"

"Well, Mother, there was this poor old woman," and the girl stopped as the flowers and sapphires cascaded down to the floor. Soon there was almost a carpet around her feet, flowers with sweet smells and jewels that sparkled.

"Aren't they lovely?" she said, picking up a rose and holding it to her nose. But her mother and sister were pushing aside the flowers and picking up the jewels. So she bent down and gathered all the flowers and put them in a big vase. "They are so pretty," she said, admiring them, for she loved flowers. Their scent filled the room.

All day, flowers and jewels fell from her lips as the young girl spoke. Soon her greedy mother and sister had a box filled with jewels, and the young girl a room full of flowers. "*You* must go and fetch the water tomorrow," the mother told her elder daughter.

"What! Me?" the elder girl said in a rage. "I am not going to fetch water. That's *her* job!" And she tossed her head, twisting pearls in her hair and looking at herself in the mirror.

"Don't be silly! Of course you will fetch the water. Look what present you might be given!" said her mother. So her elder daughter smiled and thought of the riches she would have next day.

In the morning she refused to take the heavy bucket. "She can do that later." She picked up a small silver jug. That would be enough for her to carry. She set off, grumbling, to the well.

She was too lazy to lower the bucket, to get fresh water, and she filled her jug from the stale water that was already in it. As she did so, she heard footsteps. A tall, finely dressed lady was by her side. This was the same fairy who had been at the well the day before, in a disguise. She wondered if this girl too was sweet-tempered.

"May I have a drink of your water please?" she asked as the girl lifted the jug.

"Certainly not!" replied the girl with a toss of her head. "Do you think I came to the well to get water for you? Get it yourself!" And she picked up her jug and glared at the lady.

"Can't you spare me one drop please?" the lady asked again.

"Be off with you!" the girl said rudely. "If you want water, there's the bucket!" And she turned away.

"You are rude and bad tempered," said the lady softly. "But I will give you a gift all the same." At this the girl preened and simpered. She would get gold and silver she was sure!

"The gift is not one you will like, but it is your own fault. From now on, every time you open your mouth, a toad or a snake will fall out. That is my gift to you!" And with that, the lady disappeared.

The elder girl ran home, water spilling from her jug as she ran. Her mother was waiting.

"Well, what happened? Was the old woman there?" she asked. She could not wait to see the present. Maybe it would be gold!

"Oh, Mother," the girl began, "there was a woman, not a beggar, but a fine lady."

But as she spoke, a green viper and an ugly, slimy toad dropped from her lips!

"Oh, oh!" she cried, holding up her skirts, and two more dropped to the ground.

"Help!" cried her mother, brushing them away. "What have you done? Mercy me!"

"I am sorry," the poor girl tried to say, but so many toads and snakes fell and twisted and writhed at her feet, she climbed on to a chair.

"It's all your fault!" said the mother to her younger daughter. "It's all your doing!" And she chased her out of the house into the woods.

Afraid and lonely, the poor girl wandered in the woods. Then one day along came a fine prince on a magnificent charger.

"I'm lost, fair maiden," he said. "Can you help me?"

"Gladly, if I can," she smiled and said. And, as she spoke jewels and flowers fell all around her. The prince was enchanted with her.

"Will you marry me?" he asked, lifting her on to his horse.

"Gladly," she replied, and more jewels and flowers fell from her lips.

So the young girl and the prince were married and lived happily ever after. As for her sister, she wandered in the forest but no prince ever came to fall in love with her.

# Cinderella

There was, long, long ago, a rich merchant whose wife had died. He lived alone with his pretty daughter. Then he married again, choosing a woman with two daughters of her own. He thought they would be friends with his own child. How wrong he was! His new wife was selfish and loved only her own daughters, who were plain and dull. Soon, they were jealous of the pretty child, and made her do all the housework. All day long she toiled in the big house, polishing and scrubbing, brushing and dusting from morning until dusk. Her father paid no attention!

"Bring us some more cake!" her stepsisters would order as they lay in bed.

"Pass us our clothes," and they would preen and primp in front of their mirrors, deciding which of their many dresses to wear.

No one bothered about the little girl whose own clothes grew so shabby they were in rags. At night, she was so tired she curled up by the embers of the fire to keep warm, so her stepsisters gave her the name of Cinderella.

"Great news, great news, my children!" the merchant said one day. A messenger from the king had arrived inviting the girls to a great ball at the Palace in honour of the Prince's birthday. All the nobility of the land would be there, and people of importance, so the stepmother and her daughters spent hours deciding what to wear.

Dressmakers were sent for, and rolls and rolls of silks and satins and fine cloths were held up for them to choose.

"I think I shall have velvet!" said one sister, holding up a roll of rich red material. "See how its softness flatters my looks!" And she rubbed her face against the roll.

"I prefer brocade," said her sister. "It will give me dignity, and show off my fine profile." And the elder sister twirled and twisted this way and that with the material.

At long last, the great day came. The dressmakers, with pins falling from their lips, came for last minute fittings. The two girls squirmed and gazed in front of the mirrors, and poor Cinderella was running hither and thither, fastening this and fixing that. Everything had to be just right for so great an occasion. The hairdressers had left, one in tears because the sisters were so fussy, and the dresses were ready to wear. Cinderella helped her sisters until they looked very fine.

"How would you like to go to the ball?" they asked her, falling about with laughter. The idea! Cinderella at the ball! Whatever next!

"Come on, we shall be late," the merchant called the girls to the coach, and off they went in a flurry of silks and satins. Cinderella watched them go with an ache in her heart. How she would love to go to the ball! She crept back to her place by the fireside and began to cry. Then she heard a faint knocking at the back door. Drying her eyes, Cinderella opened it. An old woman in a tattered cloak stood there.

"Why are you crying, child?" she asked.

"I am crying because . . ." Cinderella said, and stopped. What was the use? "It doesn't matter," she said.

"There's no need to tell me," said the old lady. "I know why you are crying. You want to go to the ball!"

Cinderella looked at her. How could she know?

"I'm your fairy godmother," the old woman told her. "If you do as I tell you, you can go to the ball. Now go into the garden and bring me the biggest pumpkin you can find. Hurry!" And she gave her a little push.

Cinderella ran into the garden and brought in the biggest pumpkin she could find. Her godmother touched it with her stick, and, hey presto, there stood a magnificent coach!

"Good, now for the horses to pull it," said her godmother. "Go and look in the pantry and bring me the mice in the traps there."

Sure enough, there were six white mice in the traps. Cinderella freed them and gave them to her godmother. Another touch with her stick and each mouse was changed into a prancing white horse.

"We will need a coachman," the godmother went on, "see if you can find a rat in the trap."

So Cinderella brought a fine rat with long whiskers and, with a touch, he turned into a coachman with a livery, brass buttons and a three cornered hat.

"All you need now are the footmen!" said her godmother. "Go and look by the watering can. There should be some lizards there."

A moment later and six lizards, blinking in the firelight, had been turned into six splendid footmen with blue livery and white wigs. They looked as if they had always been footmen. One of them even held the coach door open.

"Well, now you can go to the ball," said her godmother. "Hurry up or you will miss the dancing."

"But how can I go like this?" said Cinderella. "I have no dress to wear. I can't go in rags."

"Oh, is that all!" The godmother touched the tip of Cinderella's skirt with her stick and, before she could blink, Cinderella felt her rags slip away and she was wearing the most beautiful ball gown in all the world. The dress was white, with gold and silver threads, there was a diamond necklace round her throat, and even her hair was perfect, piled high on her head and threaded with pearls that gave a soft sheen as she moved. Cinderella could not believe her eyes.

"Here are the shoes," said her godmother holding out the prettiest, daintiest pair of glass slippers in the world.

"Is it really me?" gasped Cinderella, as she slipped them on. She was ready. She smiled and stepped into her coach, the footman tucking a rug round her as he closed the door.

"Just one more thing," her godmother called. "Enjoy yourself, but do not stay one second after midnight. My magic will not work when the clock strikes twelve. You must be home by then."

"I will," promised Cinderella, and she was soon speeding in her coach along the road to the Palace. In the distance, she could hear music and see the lights flickering in the trees. Her feet tapped to the

music. She had never felt so excited!

When the Prince heard that a most beautiful princess had arrived he ran to greet her, and escorted Cinderella from her coach to the ballroom. There he danced every dance with her. He had never seen anyone so beautiful, and he fell in love with her at once.

"Who is she?" everyone was whispering, but no one knew the answer. Cinderella sat near her stepsisters at supper, even passing them a dish of tiny, sugared fruit, but they did not know her.

So the evening wore on and it was nearly midnight. Cinderella was so happy she forgot her godmother's warning until she heard the first stroke of midnight boom out. Daaang! went the huge clock.

Cinderella made a deep curtsy to the King and Queen and ran down the wide, wide staircase out into the night.

In her haste, she dropped one of her slippers, but she did not dare to stop and pick it up. As the clock stopped striking, Cinderella's dress turned to rags, the coach and horses had disappeared, and all that remained was a large rat who stroked his whiskers before slinking away into the darkness. Trembling, Cinderella ran home and curled up by the fire, thinking about her evening.

When she heard her stepsisters return, she ran to help them. They could not stop talking about the ball and the beautiful Princess who had danced with the Prince all evening, and then disappeared. Cinderella smiled but said nothing.

Next day at the palace the Prince was desolate. None had seen the lovely Princess leave. No one knew her name. All he had was the glass slipper he had picked up on the stairs. He knew he had to find her. She was the princess he wanted to marry. He summoned his heralds.

"Take this glass slipper," he ordered, "search the length and

breadth of the kingdom if you must, but find me the Princess whose foot it fits.''

So they travelled far and wide searching and asking every girl in the land. All tried on the slipper but it fitted none. On the third day, the Prince himself went with the heralds, calling at every household. First one, then another girl tried the slipper but it was no use. At last they came to the merchant's house. The stepsisters were beside themselves with excitement.

"Let me try it on," said the first snatching the slipper in her haste. Her sister stood behind her. "Hurry, hurry!" she said. "It's going to fit me!"

The first stepsister could not get her toe into the slipper and demanded a knife to cut it off. But her sister was too impatient for her turn.

"Don't be silly," she cried, "give it to me!"

No matter how much she struggled and pushed, the slipper was too small. Sadly, she put it down.

The Prince looked at the merchant who was bowing low. "Have you any other daughters?" he asked.

"Well, there's my own daughter, but I hardly think . . ." said the merchant doubtfully.

"Send for her!" insisted the Prince, and shyly Cinderella came into the room in her rags. She sat down and tried on the slipper which, of course, fitted perfectly. From her pocket she brought out the other.

Just at that moment her fairy godmother arrived, and touched Cinderella with her stick once more. And there stood the beautiful Princess of the night before. The Prince was overwhelmed with joy. He had found his Princess.

In a few days they were married and lived happily ever after. As for the stepsisters, Cinderella gladly forgave them.

# The Ridiculous Wishes

**A** poor woodcutter and his wife lived in a cottage on the edge of the
forest. Life was very hard, for they had no money. The man grumbled
and grumped all day long.

"Sometimes," he would say, "sometimes, I think I would be better
off dead! I work all day till I am fit to drop. But there is no reward for
me. Oh, how I hate life."

His wife was just the same. As she went about the little cottage,
cleaning and dusting, she would say to herself, "What is the good of all
this? I work all day, trying to make a meal for us to eat, and we are still
hungry. There is no sense at all in all this." And she would shake her
head and moan about her miserable life.

One day, while he was chopping a tree, the woodcutter stopped to
take breath and have a little grumble. He heard a rustling in the leaves
and a tiny wizard stood beside him.

"Oh, dearie me," the wizard said, "never have I heard such
grumbles! Day after day, you and your wife, grumble, grumble,
grumble! I tell you, I am sick and tired of listening to you."

"Well, we have plenty to complain about," said the woodcutter
crossly, picking up his axe.

"I have decided to help you," said the wizard. "Listen very
carefully. I will give you three wishes."

"Three wishes!" said the woodcutter in surprise.

"Yes, three wishes," said the wizard, "but let me warn you. Use
them well, for your future depends on it!" And he was gone as swiftly
as he had come.

The woodcutter threw down his axe and hurried home to tell his
wife the news.

"Wife," he called, "come and sit down. Something wonderful has
happened." And they sat down at the table, she with her duster in her
hand, ready to listen.

When he told her the news, the woodcutter's wife was thinking of all the pretty dresses she would like. She stood up and twirled round as if she were wearing one already.

"Steady," said the woodcutter. "Remember what he said. Let's have a glass of wine, and think about this very carefully."

So he poured them both a glass of wine from the bottle on the table and they sat down. For a long time there was a silence, each was busy with their own thoughts. The wife was still thinking of lovely dresses, and then curtains and carpets for the cottage. The woodcutter wanted a new axe with a keener edge to make his work less hard. He sipped his wine.

"I wish I had some sausage to go with this!" he said out loud.

Before the words had scarce left his mouth, a great, big, juicy sausage landed on the table, right in front of him!

"Oh, you fool!" shouted his wife. "Fancy wishing for a sausage when you could have gold, silver—oh, anything! I despair of you! What shall we do?" And she rapped him with her spoon she was so angry.

Though he knew he was silly to have wished for a sausage, the woodcutter grew angry. His wife went on and on. At last, when he could stand the noise no longer, he turned to her and said crossly,

"Oh, do shut up! I wish the silly sausage would stick to your nose!"

No sooner had he spoken than he heard a scream from his wife. There! At the end of her nose, was the sausage! No amount of pulling and tugging would remove it. In spite of himself, the woodcutter began to laugh, for she really did look rather funny.

"*Do* something!" she shouted but her voice was muffled as she tried to speak through her nose. She couldn't eat or drink either, the nose kept getting in her way.

The woodcutter was silent. Only one wish was left. He looked at his wife.

"I could wish I was a King in a palace," he said, "but you would not like to be a Queen with that on your face, would you?"

"No," the poor woman replied. "I'd rather be the wife of a poor woodcutter, living in a cottage on the edge of the forest."

"Very well then," said the woodcutter. "I wish your face was as it was before!"

The horrid sausage disappeared and his wife rubbed her nose thoughtfully. It felt just the same. Everything was as before. Nothing had changed. Or had it? Somehow, I don't think the woodcutter and his wife ever grumbled again.

# Little Red Riding Hood

There was once, many, many years ago, a little girl who lived in the forest. Her father was a woodcutter, and all day long, the tap-tap, tap-tap of his axe could be heard among the great trees. Her mother made the little girl a red cloak with a hood and, as she wore it every day, they all called her 'Little Red Riding Hood'.

One day her mother said to her, "Your grandmother is not very well. I want you to take this basket and go and visit her in her cottage. Carry it carefully, there's some eggs, and custard and the little cakes she enjoys. Remember, go straight there, and, whatever you do, don't leave the path."

"Yes Mother," said Little Red Riding Hood. And she put on her cloak and hood, and, holding the basket very carefully so as not to drop anything, she set off along the path.

It was a lovely day with the sun shining, and Little Red Riding Hood sang as she walked along. She felt very important to be visiting her grandmother.

"I'll just stop and pick her some flowers," she said, for she was a kind little girl. And she turned a little off the path to gather some bluebells by the side. She did not know that a great big wolf was following her!

"Where are you going, my dear?" he asked, stepping out in front of her.

Little Red Riding Hood was afraid, but she stood still. "I'm going to see my poor grandmother who is ill," she said. "I am taking her this food and these flowers."

"Where does your Grannie live?" asked the wolf, licking his lips.

"Her cottage is just a little further on along this path. I'm nearly there," she said. And she went on her way.

The wolf ran on ahead, dodging in and out of the trees. He knew the cottage well, and, taking a short cut, was there long before Little Red Riding Hood. He rapped at the door.

"Who is there?" asked a voice.

"It's me, Little Red Riding Hood," said the wolf in a whisper. "Let me in. I've brought you some cakes."

"Open the latch, my dear," said a voice, "it's not locked."

Then the grandmother saw the wolf! "What a fright you gave me!" she cried, and ran to hide in the cupboard. Though the wolf banged on the door, he could not get in. But he had no time to waste. The little girl would be a much tastier morsel anyway.

Quickly, he found an old nightie and cap belonging to Grannie and, putting them on, crept into bed. Her glasses lay on the side table. He put them on at the end of his nose. He picked up a mirror and looked at his face. He was rather pleased. He thought he looked just like a grandmother!

Very soon, Little Red Riding Hood reached the cottage. She rapped on the door with her knuckles.

"Who is there?" asked the wolf in a crackly voice.

"It's me, Little Red Riding Hood," said the little girl. "I've come all the way to see you, and brought you some food and some flowers. May I come in?"

"Come in, come in," called the wolf. "Lift the latch, the door is not locked."

So Little Red Riding Hood lifted the latch and went inside. She hurried in, to see her grandmother sitting in bed, with the blankets up to her chin. She thought she looked very odd.

"I've picked these flowers for you," she said, holding them up.

"How kind," muttered the wolf, "put them in a vase where I can see them." So Little Red Riding Hood found some water and put them in a vase, just where her grannie could see them.

"Put the food in the pantry, and come and sit beside me," said the wolf. And Little Red Riding Hood came and sat on the big bed gazing at her grandmother.

"Oh, Grannie, what big ears you have!" she said, staring at her.

"All the better to hear you with," said the wolf.

"But Grannie, what great big eyes you have!" said Little Red Riding Hood.

"All the better to see you with," said the wolf.

"And Grannie what great big arms you have!" said Little Red Riding Hood, for the wolf's paws had slipped out of the blankets.

"All the better to hug you with," said the wolf, trying to seize Little Red Riding Hood.

"But Grannie, your teeth—I have never seen such big teeth!" gasped Little Red Riding Hood.

"All the better to eat you with!" snarled the wolf, springing from the bed.

Little Red Riding Hood screamed! Then a woodcutter, passing by, who had seen the wolf about, rushed in, fought it, and killed it! Just then, Grannie came out of the cupboard and hugged and hugged Little Red Riding Hood, who had had a terrible fright.

The kindly woodcutter walked home with Little Red Riding Hood after they had shared the little cakes and custards that she had brought for her grandmother. Little Red Riding Hood often went to visit her grandmother, but she never met another wolf.